W9-BUS-286

DATE DUE

Ernest and Elston

Ernest Series ®

Ernest and Elston is part of the Ernest Series.®

Barnesyard Books and Ernest are trademarks of Barnesyard Books, Inc.

2005© Laura T. Barnes and Barnesyard Books, Inc.

Book design by Christine Wolstenholme

Published by Barnesyard Books, Inc., Sergeantsville, NJ 08557
www.barnesyardbooks.com

Printed in China

Library of Congress Catalog Card Number: 2005900628

ISBN 0-9674681-6-7

Ernest and Elston

by Laura T. Barnes

Illustrated by Carol A. Camburn

BARNESYARD BOOKS ®

Sergeantsville, NJ 08557 • www.barnesyardbooks.com

For my parents – who made everything possible.

– L.T.B

For my brothers, Charlie and Ron, and in memory of Pop.

– C.A.C.

It was very, very early morning on the farm.
It was still dark and peaceful.

Elston, the rooster, stood up on his perch. He looked around the quiet barn.
Although the animals were standing, it was clear that they were in a deep sleep.

The handsome rooster peeked outside and saw a yellow crack beginning to surface at the edge of the sky.
It was time.

Elston ruffled his brightly colored feathers.

He proudly puffed out his broad chest, leaned back and let out a loud, "Cockle doodle do."

He quickly leaned back again and uttered another ear splitting, "Cockle doodle doooo."

"Cockle doodle doooooo!" he screeched one last time, satisfied that his job was done.

Slowly the horses, cows and donkeys started to wake up. They stretched back and forth and yawned.

"Ugh," moaned the sleepy donkey. "Why do you have to make that racket every morning?"

"I'm not sure," answered Elston. "I just do, do, do...." and with that he uttered another extra loud, "Cockle doodle dooooooooo."

"Just one morning, I'd like to sleep in," yawned the horse. "Just one morning I'd like it to be quiet."

"I'm sorry, I can't help myself," explained Elston.

The rooster didn't want the animals to be mad.
He wanted them to like him. He hid his beak in his
feathers and huddled in the corner.

Ernest, the little miniature donkey, walked over to Elston.
"Don't worry Elston. Your crowing doesn't bother me."

"Well it bothers everybody else. They don't like me," stated Elston.

"Just because you crow and wake them up,
doesn't mean they don't like you," explained Ernest.

"I wish I could stop crowing. Maybe they'd like me then," Elston said sadly.

"But they do like you!" repeated Ernest.

The little donkey was extra tiny, but he had a very big heart.

He knew what it was like to be different from the others. Ernest tried to help his friend understand.

"Elston your crow is what makes you special. That's what roosters do."

"I don't like being a rooster. And I'm not going to crow anymore," claimed Elston.

"Don't be silly," said Ernest. "Come on, let's go outside with the others."

Ernest trotted out of the stall with Elston running closely behind.

They all headed to the pond. Elston tried to keep up. He ran as fast as he could.
The donkeys were only walking yet, they were much faster than he was.

"They run so fast. It must be because they have two more legs than I do.
I wish I was more like them," thought Elston.

"Just look at all these feathers. I wish I had a furry
coat like a donkey. What good are feathers?"

And with that, Elston rolled in the mud by the pond. He rolled and rolled
trying to hide his feathers by covering them with dirt.

"There, that's better," mumbled Elston. "Now at
least I'm almost the same color as them."

"Yikes, what happened to you?" asked a surprised Ernest.

"I covered up my feathers," explained Elston.

"Why would you want to do that?" questioned Ernest. "Your feathers are beautiful."

"I want to be like you. I want to be a donkey!" stated Elston.

"But you're not a donkey. You're a rooster! Just be you," assured Ernest.

"But I wake everybody up in the morning, and I'm different," sighed Elston.
"I don't like being a rooster. Being a rooster is for the birds!"

Ernest chuckled, "But that's what makes you special."

Ernest didn't know what to say to cheer up Elston. After all, Elston wasn't meant to be a
donkey and he never would be. Ernest liked his friend just the way he was.

Elston's feathers were getting heavy as the mud began to dry in the sun.
He waddled back to the barn to hide in the shade of the stall.

Elston's wings were so heavy he couldn't fly up onto his perch.

Exhausted, he huddled by the hay bales and went to sleep.

He was so tired that he slept through the afternoon and straight through the night.

The next morning as the sun started to rise, Elston woke up. His chest started to swell for his morning crow.

"Oh no," worried Elston, "I am *not* going to crow and wake everyone up."

Elston stuffed his beak in the hay bale to prevent himself from crowing. He held his breath. He felt like he was going to burst. His whole body puffed up trying to stifle his crow.

It took all of his effort to not do what came naturally to him.

Finally the urge to crow passed. The effort wore him out and he fell back to sleep.

Ernest and the others were still fast asleep. Hours passed. The animals slept and slept.

It was almost noon when Ernest started to open his eyes. He stretched and yawned and looked around. The sun was shinning brightly in the sky. Everyone else was still asleep.

"What's going on?" he wondered. He shook his head so that he was wide awake. He looked over near the hay. He saw that Elston was still asleep, too.

"Elston! Elston!" he called. "Elston!" shouted Ernest even louder. "Look what happens when you don't act like a rooster. Nobody woke up! Don't try to be someone you're not. You're a rooster. We need you to be *you*!"

"I didn't know you needed me," said Elston with a sleepy smile.

"Well, we do! We need you to crow and wake us up in the morning," explained Ernest.
"We can't start our day without you."

"I need your help now," instructed Ernest. "Help me wake the others."

"How?" asked Elston.

"Crow! Crow and crow and crow," pleaded Ernest.

"But I can't crow *now*," said Elston.

"You've got to try," begged Ernest.
"Otherwise, nobody is going to wake up. Come on Elston, please try."

"Well, maybe I can." Elston stood up and shook off the remaining dirt from his feathers. He shook and shook. The mud started to crack and flake off of his feathers. Elston flapped his wings, loosening the final pieces of dirt.

He stuck out his chest and crowed meekly, "Cockle doodle do."

Then Elston leaned back, flapped his beautiful feathers and crowed and crowed,
"Cockle doodle doo! Cockle doodle doooooo!"

The animals opened their eyes and began to yawn.

Ernest smiled. "Yea for Us! Everyone is awake. Yea for Us!"

Elston continued with his magnificent crow. His crow got louder and louder, "Cockle doodle doooooo!"

The animals hadn't realized how much they needed Elston.
The beautiful rooster was an important part of their farm. They could not start their day without him.

"See, you *are* different," explained Ernest. "But you're perfect just the way you are. You're just as you're meant to be."

Elston laughed, "Thank goodness I'm different so that I can help you wake up to enjoy a new day."

Laughing, the circle of friends headed outside. They had already missed half of their day. They didn't want to miss a minute more.